To our daughter, Alexandra

Town Book Press
255 East Broad Street
Westfield, NJ 07090

Town Book Press is an imprint of
The Town Book Store of Westfield, Inc.

Printed in Korea

10 9 8 7 6 5 4 3 2 1

ISBN 1-892657-00-7

Library of Congress Catalog Card Number: 98-86646

HOW FLETCHER WAS HATCHED

By Wende and Harry Devlin

Town Book Press
Westfield, NJ

*A*lexandra sat in the sunlight watching a chick hatch from an egg.

"Peep!" and it was out of its shell.

"Fletcher," she called to her dog, "look at this dear chick. It's so tiny. It's so yellow. It's so fluffy!"

"It's so stupid," growled Fletcher to himself. He gave Alexandra a hopeless look and walked to his water dish. It was empty. Another thing – he hadn't had his ears scratched in days. "No one wants a first-rate hound dog around here," he thought to himself. "She's forgotten me." Fletcher raised his head and howled miserably.

"Quiet, noisy! The chicks are sleeping." Alexandra
turned her back on Fletcher.

With a wounded look, Fletcher shuffled mournfully away toward the park at the edge of town. At the far end of the park was a pond where Fletcher's faithful friends, Beaver and Otter, lived.

Otter was splashing Beaver at the water's edge when Fletcher shuffled up. The animals weren't long in noticing Fletcher's sadness. Fletcher saw to that with a few deep moans and some very loud sniffles. Alarmed, they gathered close to hear his tale.

"She's forgotten me," said Fletcher. "She loves chickens. Cute, fluffy, peeping, STUPID chickens."

Beaver and Otter, who were wild, free animals, didn't really understand Fletcher's deep attachment to his mistress, but they understood that Fletcher was terribly unhappy.

"I'm terribly unhappy," said Fletcher.

"Maybe if you were fluffy and yellow . . ." said Otter doubtfully.

"Could you peep-peep a little?" asked Beaver.

"If you could only hatch once in a while," said Otter.

"That's it!" cried Beaver, slapping his tail. "We'll have you hatch. It will be a new beginning!"

"Me – hatch?" yelped Fletcher.

But Beaver and Otter paid little attention to Fletcher. They were soon in a warm discussion of how to make an egg large enough to hold a hound dog.

With some misgivings, Fletcher promised to do his part and act like a chicken.

They built the egg around Fletcher. All day they
worked in the sun with reeds, clay and river grasses.

Otter sometimes stopped to tickle Fletcher's nose
with a cornflower, but Beaver, who was a master
builder, worked steadily, plastering pink clay evenly
over a reed network.

With his friends working so tirelessly, Fletcher
couldn't complain, even when wet lumps of clay
dropped on his head.

At last it was finished. Beaver had smoothed the clay over the surface with such artistry that there could be little doubt that this great, pink, pearly object was an egg – an egg that would have been a joy to any mother bird's heart. He speckled it brown in honor of Fletcher's own brown spots.

Two small holes were left in the egg so that Fletcher could be fed water and a strawberry or two.

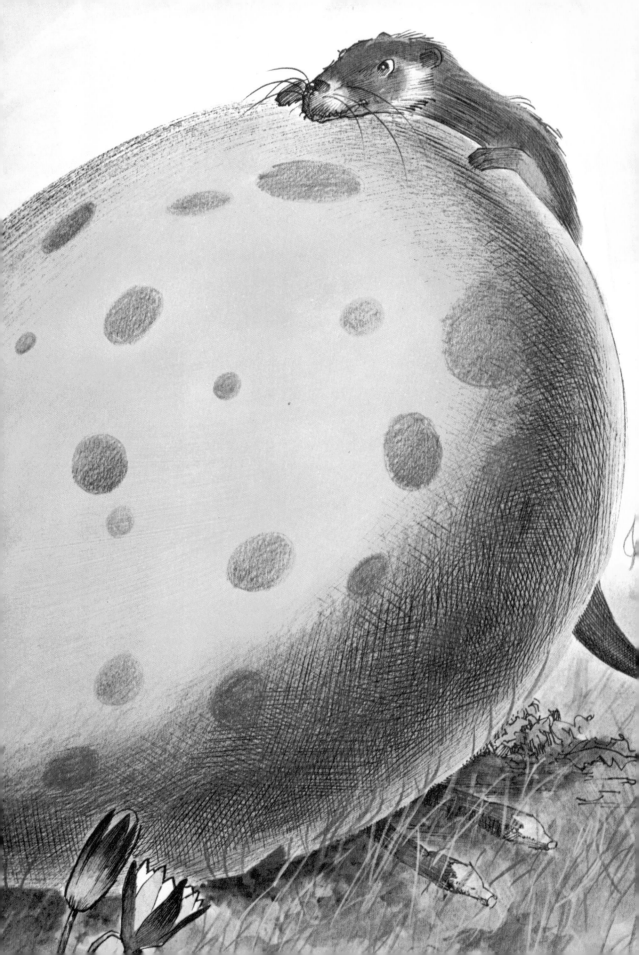

Beaver, Otter and Fletcher were tired. It had been a long day's work. Shadows grew deeper and lengthened into the blue of night, and when the pumpkin-colored moon appeared on the rim of the pond, Beaver and Otter, nestling close to their great egg, lay deep in sleep.

Inside the egg, feeling very homesick, Fletcher wondered if Alexandra was thinking of him.

Back in the farmhouse, Alexandra lay awake under her red quilt. Tears fell on her pillow. How could she sleep with Fletcher gone, perhaps never to return? The clock struck twelve before she finally went off to sleep.

At last it was morning. At the pond the white surface of the water was broken by jumping frogs and leaping minnows. Otter and Beaver awoke and ambled down to the water's edge for a quick dip and breakfast.

They didn't forget a few strawberries for Fletcher, who was discovering that the inside of an egg is a most unsatisfactory place to yawn and stretch.

"Let's go," commanded Beaver. Now the animals started the last part of their plan. Very carefully they pushed, shoved and rolled the egg until they reached a large clump of grass by the path that led to Alexandra's school. Inside the egg Fletcher felt a bit bruised and very confused.

The town began to wake up slowly and the sounds of traffic drove Beaver and Otter back to the pond and the tall grasses.

They shouted goodbye

"Good luck, Fletch, and remember, no barking – just peeping."

"Peep, " growled Fletcher and then lay quiet.

It was the custodian on the way to open the school who first discovered the amazing egg.

He shouted to some nearby children. "It's an egg! The biggest one in the world! Call the science teacher."

Soon a crowd of children gathered about. Their eyes were filled with wonder.

"Where is its mother?" asked little Tommy.

"Its mother would be as large as a house," said round-eyed Gabby, shaking her blonde hair.

"Bigger," said Robert.

The science teacher scurried up to the crowd with his friend, Professor Schnitzer from the University.

The crowd became larger and members of the school band, on their way for an early practice, gathered close.

The science teacher stood up on a park bench and shouted, "Don't touch it! It looks like a Flat-Billed Prehistoric Scratchafratch. A priceless find!"

A respectful hush fell on the crowd.

"Or perhaps it is the Web-Footed Pickel-Faced Dinaflyer," cried the professor from the University.

Fletcher huddled inside the egg, quivering with excitement as he waited for Alexandra. Suddenly he heard her name. The children were telling her about the egg. Fletcher now began to get ready for the big moment, but Alexandra was making funny noises. Alexandra was crying. She told them all that she didn't want to see a stupid old egg. She was looking for lost Fletcher. In fact, the only thing in the world that she wanted was Fletcher.

Then and there Fletcher knew it was time to hatch.
He pushed and stretched and with a rising howl he
fairly exploded out of the egg.

The crowd screamed and moved back.
Fletcher shook himself and the mud flew.
Feeling that something was expected of him, he
turned to Alexandra.
"Peep!" he croaked.

Laughing and crying, Alexandra hugged him.
The two men of science looked at their shoes and
felt a little foolish.

"Strike up the band," said the principal, hoping that everyone had forgotten about his guess – that the mother of the egg was a giant hen from Mars.

The band played *Hurrah for the Red, White and Blue.* The principal, feeling called upon to bring the occasion to a close, faced the audience. He wiped his face with his handkerchief.

"Only in America," he announced with great feeling, "could a hound dog hatch!"

This seemed to please everyone. With much clapping and whistling, the crowd began to fall away.

Alexandra skipped along with Fletcher. Fletcher
panted happily. Sometimes Alexandra had to stop
to hug her dog.

And Fletcher thought to himself, "You don't have to hatch to be loved. You don't have to be yellow and peep. You can be a great hound dog with brown spots and be the most important creature in a little girl's life."

He gave himself a good shake and the last of the
dried mud on his back went flying.

By Wende & Harry Devlin

Old Black Witch

The Knobby Boys to the Rescue

Aunt Agatha, There's a Lion Under the Couch!

What's Under My Bed?

A Kiss for a Warthog

Old Witch and the Polka Dot Ribbon

Old Witch Rescues Halloween

Hang On Hester!

Cranberry Christmas

Cranberry Mystery

Cranberry Thanksgiving

Cranberry Halloween

Cranberry Valentine

Cranberry Birthday

Cranberry Easter

Cranberry Summer

Cranberry Autumn

The Trouble with Henriette

Tales From Cranberryport:

> Moving Day
>
> New Baby in Cranberryport
>
> First Day of School
>
> Maggie has a Nightmare
>
> Trip to the Dentist
>
> Lost at the Fair

By Harry Devlin

To Grandfather's House We Go: A Roadside Tour of American Homes

The Walloping Window Blind, An Old Nautical Tale

Tales of Thunder and Lightning

Portraits of American Architecture

What Kind of a House is That?